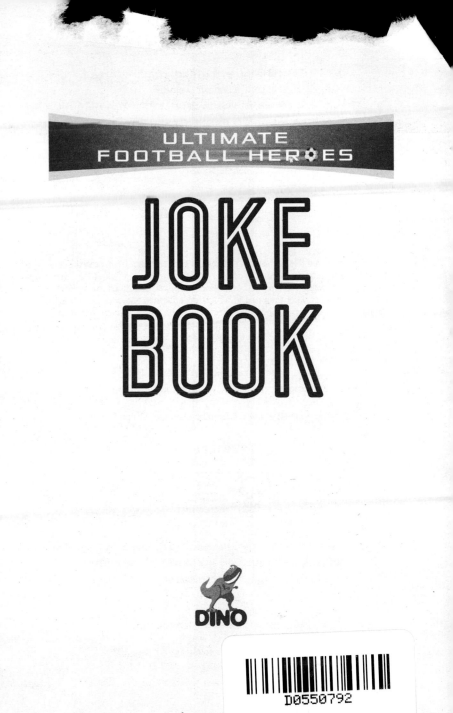

# ULTIMATE
# FOOTBALL HEROES

# JOKE
# BOOK

**DINO**

D0550792

First published by Dino Books in 2022,
an imprint of Bonnier Books UK,
4th Floor, Victoria House, Bloomsbury Square, London, WC1B 4DA
Owned by Bonnier Books,
Sveavägen 56, Stockholm, Sweden

www.bonnierbooks.co.uk

Written by Saaleh Patel
Designed by Rob Ward
Production by Nick Read

Paperback ISBN: 978 1 78946 587 7

British Library Cataloguing-in-Publication Data:
A catalogue record for this book is available from the British Library.

Printed and bound in Great Britain by Clays Ltd, Elcograf S.p.A.

1 3 5 7 9 10 8 6 4 2

All images courtesy of Shutterstock.com
PICTURE CREDITS:
Fuad Gonagov/shutterstock.com (page 80, page 103)
PJuabman/shutterstock.com (page 111)

# ULTIMATE FOOTBALL HER⚽ES

# JOKE BOOK

**DINO**

# CONTENTS

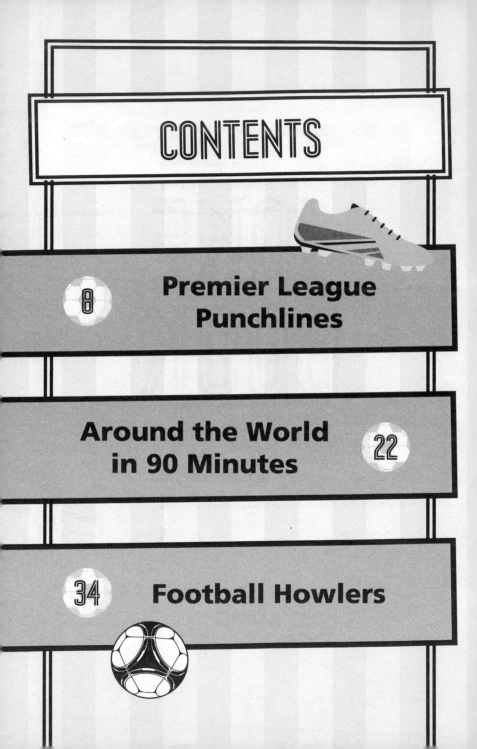

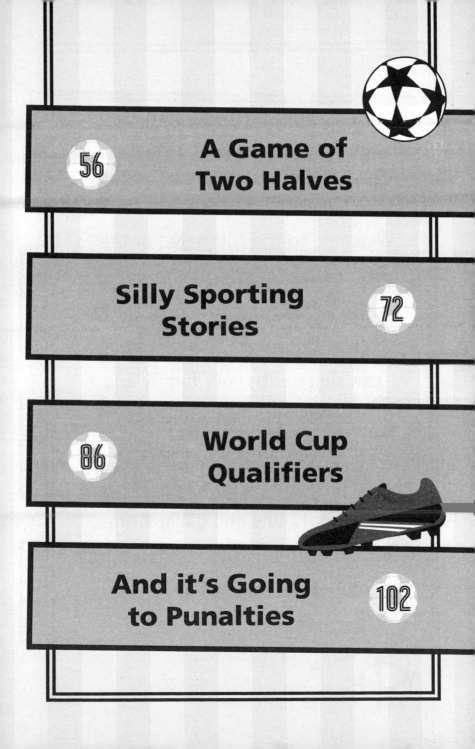

# KICK-OFF TIME!

Welcome to the Ultimate Football Heroes Joke Book! You're going to find the best of the best footy jokes in this book – jokes that you can share with your family and friends and that will leave you gasping for breath.

We've got puns and gags, stories and riddles, big LOLs and cracking one-liners all about your favourite football teams and players.

Are you ready to dive in to ninety minutes (plus stoppage time!) of football funnies?

At the whistle then...

# PREMIER LEAGUE PUNCHLINES

It's time to kick off and get stuck into the toughest league in the world!

You're going to have to deal with some head-butting, ankle-snapping, slide-tackling, rib-busting Premier League punchlines. Ready? Let's hope VAR doesn't have anything to say about it...

Why doesn't Burnley Football Club have a website?

**They can't string three W's together.**

Why were the Arsenal players given lighters?

**They kept losing their matches.**

What does an Everton fan do after winning the Premier League?

**Turns off the games console.**

What is the chilliest ground in the Premier League?

**Cold Trafford.**

What's the difference between Burnley and a tea bag?

**The tea bag stays in the cup for longer.**

Which player never turns up for work?

**A striker.**

What do you get if you cross a Premier League winning defender with a delivery man?

**Virgil VAN Driver.**

# PUNCHLINES

Can Leicester count on their midfield?

Yes Ndidi!

What's the difference between West Ham and an eagle?

An eagle has got two decent wings.

How do Arsenal fans change a lightbulb?

They don't, they just talk about how good the old one was.

**Why was Sterling covered in spit?**

*Because he was always dribbling.*

**Did you hear about the football pitch that they built on the moon?**

*They used AstroTurf.*

# PUNCHLINES

**Why do teachers from Liverpool go to Anfield in groups?**

*So They'll Never Chalk Alone.*

**What did Conte do when the pitch flooded?**

*He sent on his subs.*

**Why do the clergy support Norwich City Football Club?**

*Because they play at Vicarage Road.*

How many Everton fans does it take to screw in a lightbulb?

**None – they're quite happy living in the shadows.**

Why was Richarlison upset on his birthday?

**He got no presents, just a red card.**

Why did Sam Allardyce bring pencils and sketchbooks into the dressing room before the game?

**He was hoping for a draw!**

'**Three hours of football and Norwich's goalkeeper is still their top scorer!**'

Which team always start the match with a bang?

**The Gunners.**

What can Diogo Jota never make right?

**His left foot.**

'As Southampton's struggles continued, a pound coin was thrown onto the pitch.

Police are still trying to determine whether it was a missile or a takeover bid.'

**What's the best position to play if you don't like football?**

Right-back...right back in the changing rooms.

# PUNCHLINES

**Which team is the chewiest?**

The Toffees!

**Did you hear Mason Mount stole parts of the pitch?**

He kept taking corners.

**Why do Seagulls fans love watching their team play?**

They Brighton up their day.

# PREMIER LEAGUE

*They say that pessimists see the cup as half empty, and optimists see it as half full. Not sure what that makes Spurs, then, as they haven't even seen the cup!*

**What lights up
Stamford Bridge at night?**

*A football match.*

**What's the most royal club
in the Premier League?**

*Crystal Palace.*

# PUNCHLINES

**What is black and white and black and white and black and white?**

*A Newcastle fan rolling down a hill!*

**Which team loves retiring to bed after a game?**

*Chelsea – there's a reason they're called the Pensioners!*

**What does Theo Walcott and a judge have in common?**

*They're both on the bench.*

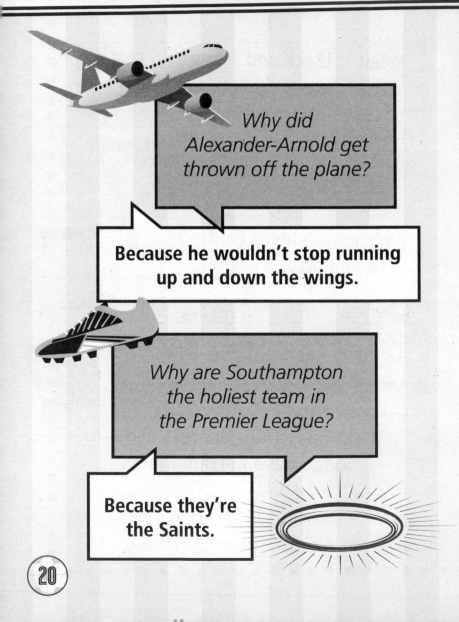

*Why did Alexander-Arnold get thrown off the plane?*

**Because he wouldn't stop running up and down the wings.**

*Why are Southampton the holiest team in the Premier League?*

**Because they're the Saints.**

# PUNCHLINES

Why can't pigs play in the Premier League?

**They hog the ball.**

What is the difference between a battery and Burnley?

**A battery has a positive side.**

What is a Newcastle fan's favourite flying bird?

**A magpie, of course!**

# AROUND THE WORLD IN 90 MINUTES

Are you ready to dive,
I mean slide, into some
great gags from across
the leagues?

You'd better be! Because
we're heading for some
stoppage time megaLOLs!

Don your jersey and
strap on your shin pads,
we're going to encounter
some famous faces
and jokesters.

**What do Lionel Messi and a magician have in common?**

*They both do hat tricks.*

**Why did the San Siro goalposts get angry?**

*Because the bar was rattled!*

**Which footballer is into hip hop?**

*Megan Rap-inoe.*

**Which ship never made it to Hull City?**

*The Champion ship.*

**Why does Neuer always stay behind to clean the pitch?**

*Because he's a sweeper.*

**Why was Sergio Busquets always cuddling his opponents?**

*Because he's a holding midfielder.*

**Why did the Bayern Munich fan wear ridiculous trousers to the game?**

*Because her dad told her that flares add to the atmosphere.*

• • • • • • • • • •

**Why do Cádiz fans plant potatoes around the edge of Nuevo Mirandilla?**

*So they have something to lift at the end of the season.*

What football club do sheep support?

**Baaaaaaaaaaaaaaaaa-rcelona.**

What did the mummy coach of Egypt say at the end of practice?

**Let's wrap this up!**

Why did Dutch winger Daniëlle van de Donk take a hosepipe to the game?

**So she could spray passes!**

Why did Leroy Sané stand by the gate during the entire training session?

**His manager told him to stay close to de-fence.**

Why did José Mourinho bring a double-decker to the training ground?

**So that he could teach his team to park the bus.**

Striker: I've just had a good idea for strengthening the team.

Manager: Good! When are you leaving?

Why did Marta bring string to her game?

So she could tie the score.

Which London team spends all its spare time at pop concerts?

Queens Park Ravers F.C.

# 90 MINUTES

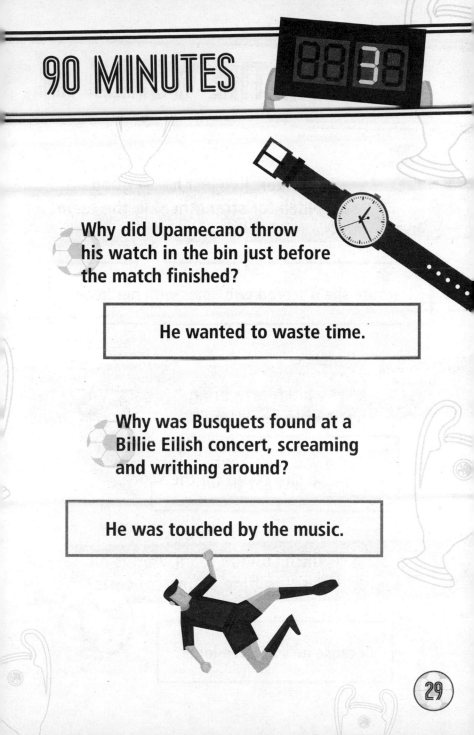

Why did Upamecano throw his watch in the bin just before the match finished?

He wanted to waste time.

Why was Busquets found at a Billie Eilish concert, screaming and writing around?

He was touched by the music.

Why did Christine Sinclair end up
in a brace after the game?

**Because she'd scored two goals with her head!**

What does Luis Suárez say to
himself before the game?

**If you can't beat
them, just eat them!**

Why doesn't Memphis Depay have
any friends to play with?

**Because he's a Barce-loner.**

Why did the head coach go to the arcade mid-game?

**He wanted his half-time change.**

Do you know why José Mourinho is a massive fan of interlocking blocks?

**Because he loves building teams.**

Which player always comes in third?

**Lucy Bronze.**

**What do PSG and the Royal Navy have in common?**

*They both spent £50 million on a sub.*

**How does Neymar laugh?**

*ROFL.*

**Why is the Estadio Monumental the coolest place to be?**

*Because it's full of fans.*

# 90 MINUTES

**Why does stellar centre-back Magdalena Eriksson visit the library every night?**

*So she can read the game even better.*

• • • • • • • • • • •

**Why did Lionel Messi throw a bucket of water on the pitch during his debut?**

*He wanted to make a big splash!*

# FOOTBALL HOWLERS

*There's nothing quite like making a right numpty of yourself and looking like a comical clown!*

*We've got some absolute howlers on the way for you – prepare to laugh (or groan…)*

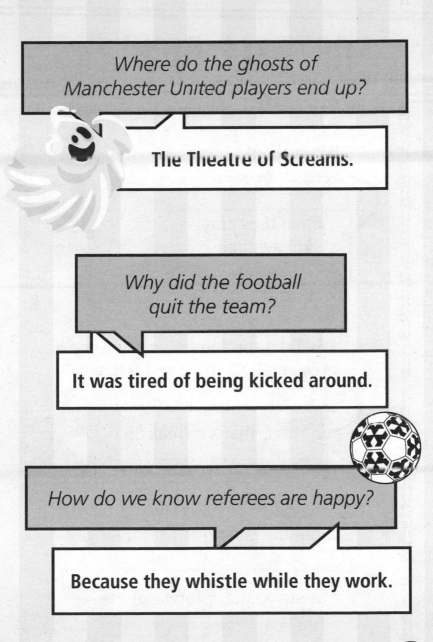

Where do the ghosts of Manchester United players end up?

The Theatre of Screams.

Why did the football quit the team?

It was tired of being kicked around.

How do we know referees are happy?

Because they whistle while they work.

# FOOTBALL HOWLERS

When should footballers wear armour?

When they play knight-time fixtures.

What did the footballer say when he accidentally burped and fell over?

Ref, that's a freak hic!

In the Greek Mythos League, who scored the most goals for their club?

The star centaur forward!

**Manager:** Twenty teams in the league and you lot finish last!

Captain: **Well, it could have been worse.**

**Manager:** How could it have been any worse?

Captain: **There could have been more teams in the league!**

**What is quick, dangerous and takes every match by a storm?**

A HarryKane!

# FOOTBALL HOWLERS

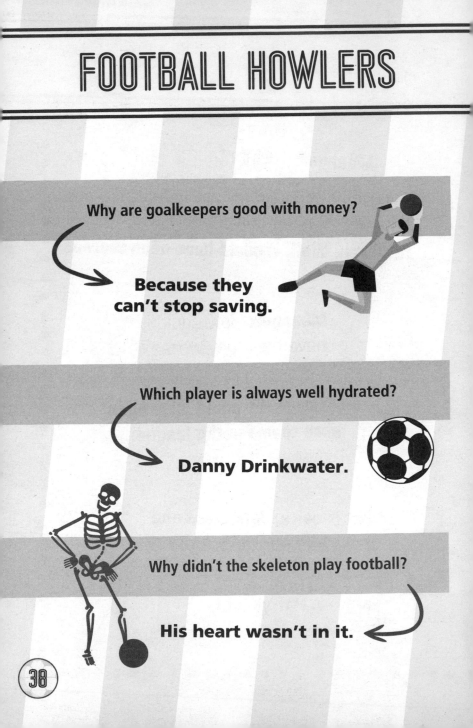

Why are goalkeepers good with money?

**Because they can't stop saving.**

Which player is always well hydrated?

**Danny Drinkwater.**

Why didn't the skeleton play football?

**His heart wasn't in it.**

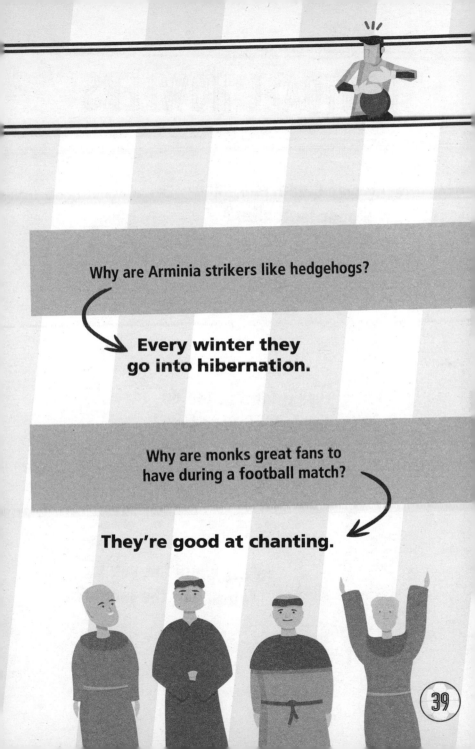

Why are Arminia strikers like hedgehogs?

**Every winter they go into hibernation.**

Why are monks great fans to have during a football match?

**They're good at chanting.**

# FOOTBALL HOWLERS

**Why was Cinderella such a poor footballer?**

*Her coach was a pumpkin.*

* * * * * * * * * *

**What kind of tea do football players love?**

*Penal-tea.*

* * * * * * * * * *

**Why shouldn't you play football in the jungle?**

*There are too many cheetahs!*

**What do scrambled eggs and the losing side have in common?**

*They've both been beaten.*

• • • • • • • •

**Why did the assistant coach buy bibs for his players on the training ground?**

*Because they kept dribbling.*

• • • • • • • • •

**Which team did Robin Hood follow?**

*Nottingham Forest.*

# FOOTBALL HOWLERS

Which player always
has some rope?

**The skipper.**

Why was the tiny ghost asked to join the football team?

**They needed a little team spirit.**

Did you hear the story about
Parrott who plays for Ireland?

**It was such a beautiful tail.**

Why do head coaches bring suitcases along to away games?

**So that they can pack the defence!**

Why was it that Robin van Persie was quickly sold when he was listed on the transfer market?

**He went cheep!**

Why was the team medic so funny?

**He kept everyone in stitches.**

# FOOTBALL HOWLERS

**Which part of the football pitch smells the nicest?**

**The scenter spot.**

**Where did the ghost kick the football?**

**Over the ghoul line!**

**What is a ghost's favourite position on the football pitch?**

**Ghoul-keeper.**

Why do footballers do well in school?

Because they know how to use their heads.

Why was the struggling manager seen shaking the club's mascot, Billy the Cat?

To check if there was any more money in the transfer kitty!

# FOOTBALL HOWLERS

**What is the difference between a bad fan and a baby?**

*The baby stops whining after a while.*

● ● ● ● ● ● ● ● ●

**Where do football directors go when they are fed up with watching their team?**

*To the bored room!*

● ● ● ● ● ● ● ● ●

**Why don't grasshoppers watch football?**

*They prefer cricket!*

**How did Scrooge end up with the football?**

*The ghost of Christmas passed.*

• • • • • • • • •

**What does a bad football team and an empty crockery cabinet have in common?**

*They have no cups.*

• • • • • • • • •

**Which team is feared by gangsters?**

*MK Dons!*

# FOOTBALL HOWLERS

Why couldn't the car play football?

It only had the one boot.

Why didn't the dog
want to play football?

It was a boxer.

Which goalkeeper can jump higher than a crossbar?

All of them, a crossbar can't jump.

How do chickens encourage their team to score?

They egg them on.

Who's the captain when fish play football?

The team's kipper!

Why aren't centipedes allowed to play football?

It takes them too long to put their boots on.

# FOOTBALL HOWLERS

Two flies are playing football on a plate.

One says to the other, 'You'd better pick up your game, Stevie.

We're playing in the cup tomorrow.'

Why aren't football grounds built in outer space?

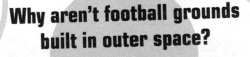

*Because there's no atmosphere.*

**Why did the footballer hold his boot to his ear?**

*Because he loved listening to sole music!*

**What is it called when a dinosaur gets a goal?**

*A dino-score.*

**What did the bumble bee say when he bagged a goal for his team?**

*'Hive scored!'*

# FOOTBALL HOWLERS

**Why couldn't the all-star footballer listen to her music?**

Because she broke all the records.

**What do you get when you cross a goalie and the Invisible Man?**

Goal tending like no one has ever seen.

**Which football team loves ice-cream?**

Aston Vanilla!

**Why is Becky Sauerbrunn so great at fishing?**

Because she has a great tackle.

**Why didn't Cinderella make it to the final?**

She always ran away from the ball.

**Are lightning bolts good at football?**

No, they're shocking!

# FOOTBALL HOWLERS

Why can't you get a cup of tea at Goodison Park?

**All the cups are at Anfield!**

What is a footballer's favourite chemical element?

**GOOOOALd!**

Leicester's Champions League fixtures next season have been announced:

**Stoke City away!**

Why was the pig ejected from the football game?

**She was playing dirty.**

What do you call a boisterous football hooligan?

**A foot-bawler.**

Which football team do cowboys support?

**Spurs!**

# A GAME OF TWO HALVES

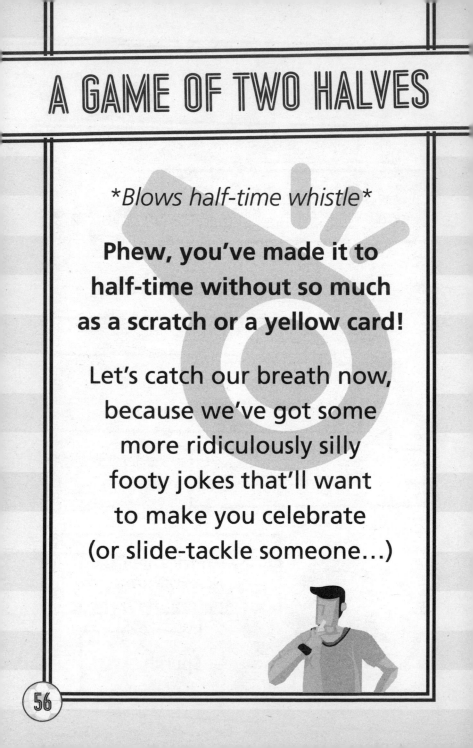

*Blows half-time whistle*

**Phew, you've made it to half-time without so much as a scratch or a yellow card!**

Let's catch our breath now, because we've got some more ridiculously silly footy jokes that'll want to make you celebrate (or slide-tackle someone...)

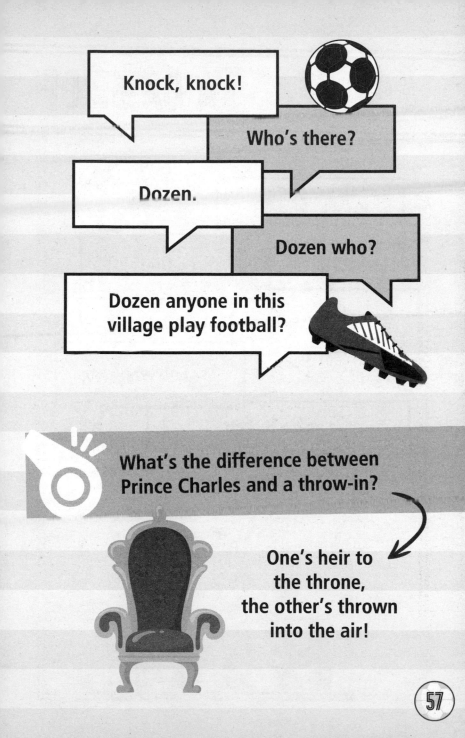

Knock, knock!

Who's there?

Les.

Les who?

Les go watch the Milan derby!

What part of the football stadium never stays the same?

The changing rooms.

Knock, knock!

Who's there?

Accrington Stanley.

Accrington Stanley who?

Exactly! Who are they?

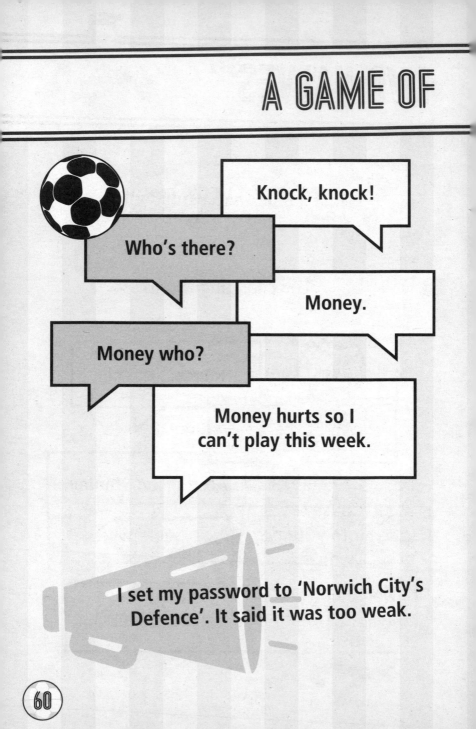

Knock, knock!

Who's there?

Money.

Money who?

Money hurts so I can't play this week.

I set my password to 'Norwich City's Defence'. It said it was too weak.

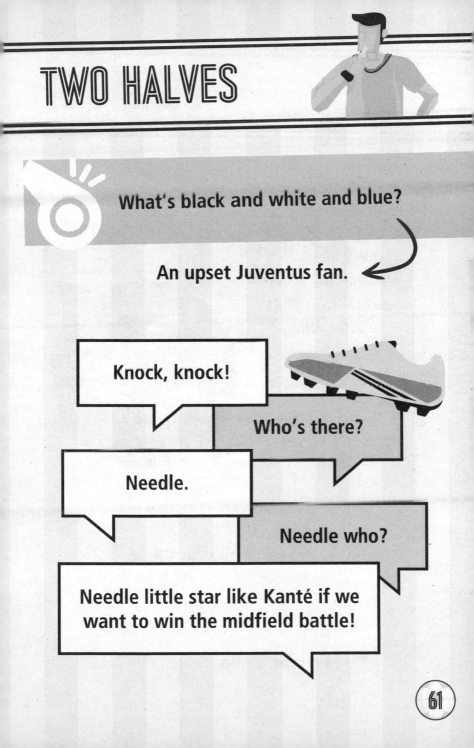

What's black and white and blue?

An upset Juventus fan.

Knock, knock!

Who's there?

Needle.

Needle who?

Needle little star like Kanté if we want to win the midfield battle!

*Manager:*
**I'll give you £50 a week to start with, and £100 a week in a year's time, okay?**

*U-18s Player:*
**Okay, I'll come back in a year's time then!**

**Did you hear about the footballer who could swim under water?**

**She was a super-sub!**

# TWO HALVES

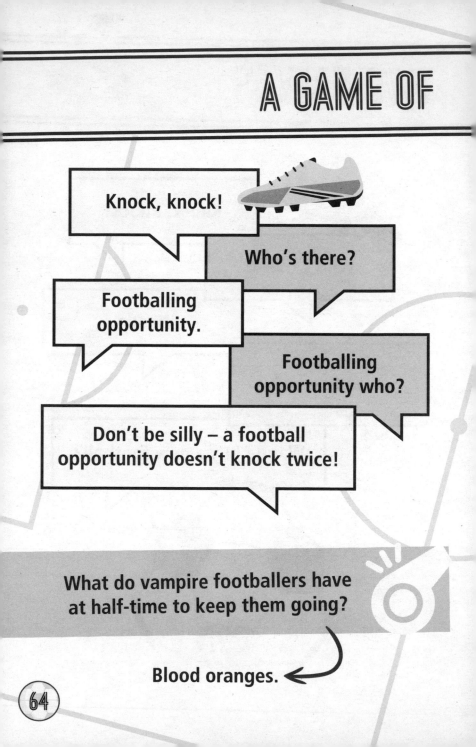

Knock, knock!

Who's there?

Footballing opportunity.

Footballing opportunity who?

Don't be silly – a football opportunity doesn't knock twice!

What do vampire footballers have at half-time to keep them going?

Blood oranges.

What do you get If you throw a kitchen sink at a team's defence?

A flat back four!

Knock, knock!

Who's there?

Mister.

Mister who?

Mister bus – that's why I'm late for training, coach!

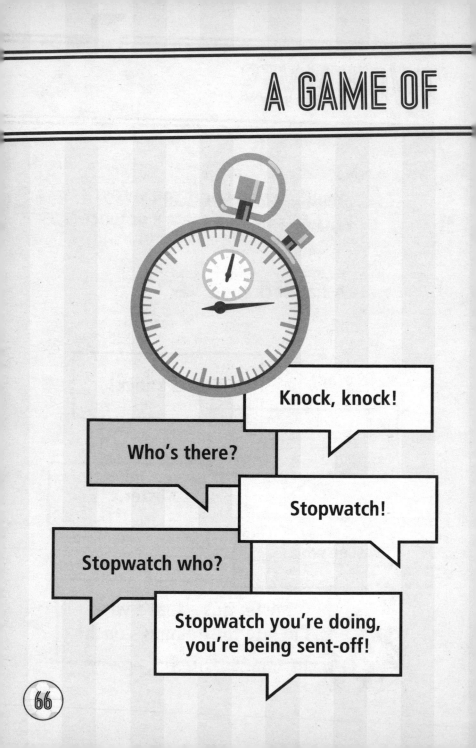

# TWO HALVES

**What is Man City's club motto?**

If at first you don't succeed,
buy, buy again.

**Did you hear about the football
team who ate too much pudding?**

They got jellygated.

**What did David Beckham's
teammates say when he was
granted a title by the Queen?**

'Man, you knighted!'

**What is a bank manager's favourite type of football?**

**Fiver side!**

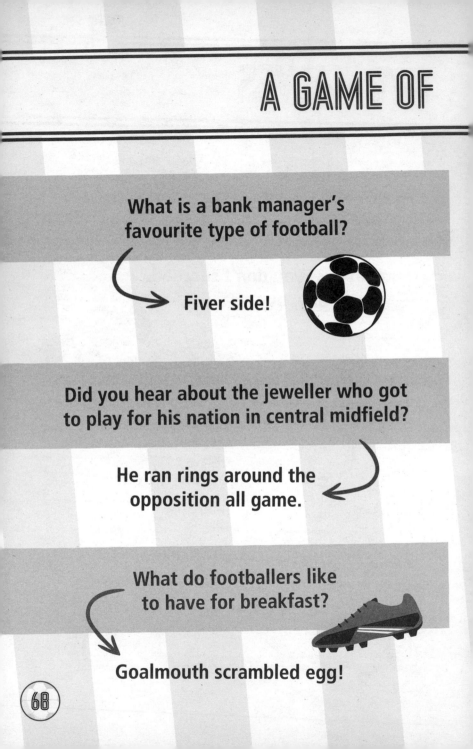

**Did you hear about the jeweller who got to play for his nation in central midfield?**

**He ran rings around the opposition all game.**

**What do footballers like to have for breakfast?**

**Goalmouth scrambled egg!**

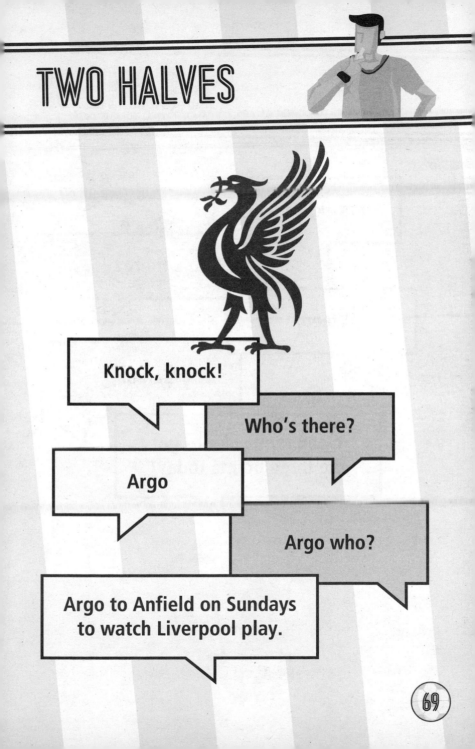

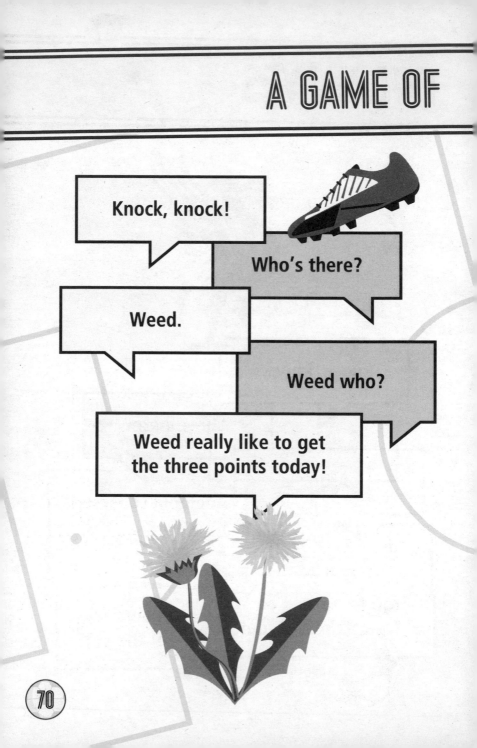

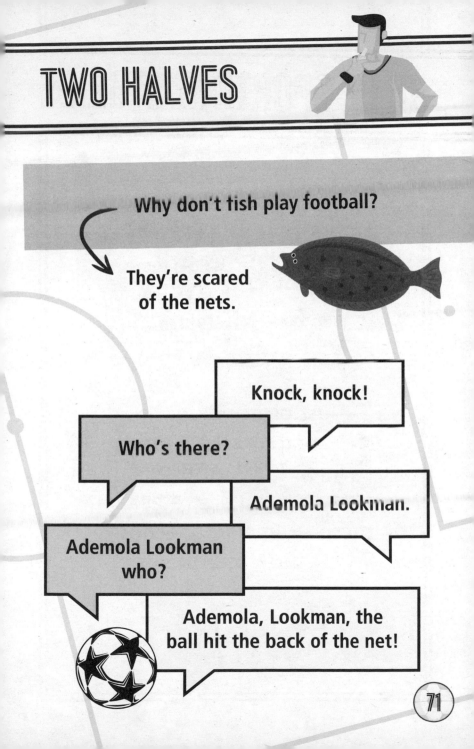

Why don't fish play football?

They're scared of the nets.

Knock, knock!

Who's there?

Ademola Lookman.

Ademola Lookman who?

Ademola, Lookman, the ball hit the back of the net!

# SILLY SPORTING STORIES

FOOTBALL STORIES MAKE FOR THE FUNNIEST OF STORIES AND WE'VE PICKED OUT SOME ABSOLUTE PEACHES FOR YOU.

Just pretend you're tuning into MNF and Jamie Carragher and Gary Neville are relaying these awesome anecdotes back to you!

Apparently, the world is going to end at 23:53 today. But if you want an extra seven minutes, go stand next to Fergie!

Simeone: 'My doctor told me I must stop playing football.'

Betty: 'Why? Is he sure? Did he examine you properly?'

Simeone: 'Not really. But he did see me playing the other week at practice.'

# SILLY SPORTING

Three friends Danny, Kassim and Tanya were talking about the sad state of their local football club:

'I blame the manager; if we could sign better players, we'd be a great club,' Danny said.

Kassim disagreed. 'I blame the players; if they made more effort, I'm sure we would score more goals.'

Tanya then stopped them both. 'I blame my parents. If I had been born in a different town, I'd be supporting a decent team!'

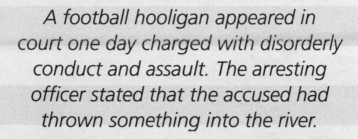

A football hooligan appeared in court one day charged with disorderly conduct and assault. The arresting officer stated that the accused had thrown something into the river.

'What exactly did the accused throw?' asked the Judge.

'Stones, your honour.'

'Well, that's hardly an offence now is it?' the Judge replied.

'It was in this case, ma'am. Stones was the referee for the game last week.'

*I was playing Football Manager when I was offered the Leeds job.*

*I knew it was a poor squad with no future, so I declined the offer immediately, then put the phone down and returned to Football Manager!*

At a fierce derby between Blackburn Rovers and Burnley last season, a spectator suddenly found herself in the thick of dozens of flying bottles and cans.

'There's nothing to worry about,' said the elderly chap standing next to her, 'it's like the bombs during the war. You won't get hit unless the bottle's got your name on it.'

'That's just what I'm worried about,' she replied, 'my name's Dr Pepper.'

*Outside the stadium corridor, just before two fans got to the turnstiles, Priya suddenly stopped in her tracks.*

**'I wish I'd brought the bedside cabinet to the stadium,' she said.**

Arun asked, 'Why would you want to bring a bedside cabinet to the football game?'

**'Because I left the tickets on it!' she exclaimed.**

I've just seen a French footballing icon playing a Nintendo™ game.

It was Thierry on Wii™.

The local team's goalkeeper asked the left-back, 'Why do you keep calling our skipper "camera"?'

He replied, 'Because he keeps snapping at me.'

*Liverpool and Manchester City's managers meet up at the end of the game in the tunnel to reflect on the result:*

'Our new winger cost fifty-five million. I call him our wonder player,' Guardiola says.

'Why's that?' asks a curious Jürgen Klopp.

'Every time he plays, I wonder why I bought him!'

A past footballer, a present footballer and a future footballer walked into a dressing room. It was tense.

*A small boy is separated from his father at a Premier League match, so he goes up to a steward and says, 'Help please, I've lost my dad!'*

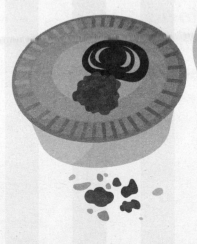

'Oh yeah? What's he like?' the steward inquires.

'Pie and chips...'

# SILLY SPORTING

Two elderly men were
holding up the queue
outside the entrance
to the stand before the
Millwall game, while
one of them hunted
for his ticket.

He looked in his coat
pockets and his cardigan
pockets and then his trouser
pockets, all to no avail.

'Hang on a minute,' said the steward, 'what's that in your mouth?'

'It's the missing ticket!' said his friend.

*As they moved inside, his mate said...*

*'Blimey, Gordon! You must be getting senile in your old age. Fancy having your ticket in your mouth and forgetting all about it!'*

'I'm not that stupid,' said Gordon, 'I was just chewing last week's date off it!'

# SILLY SPORTING

*Two fans meet
at their local chippy.*

'Do you know, Diya, I've had a season ticket at Norwich for twenty-two seasons now and I've never seen my team lose.'

'What? No way! How is that possible?' Diya responds.

'The games are so awful,
I leave at half-time!'

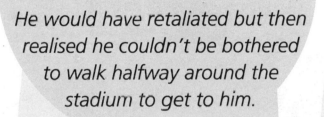

A fan was at the Man City match the other day and the fan sat closest to him called his team rubbish.

He would have retaliated but then realised he couldn't be bothered to walk halfway around the stadium to get to him.

# WORLD CUP QUALIFIERS

Make sure your laces are tied
because you're playing
on the biggest stage now!

One dodgy kick and you're
an internet meme at the World
Cup for the next four years.

It could be worse
though, you could be
the butt of a joke...

Did you hear about the Brazil manager who was always taking the squad on trips?

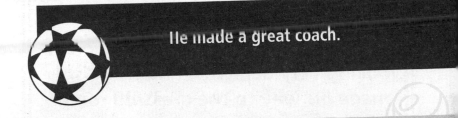

He made a great coach.

Where's the best place in the United States of America to shop for a football kit?

New Jersey.

What's the difference between The Invisible Man and San Marino?

You've got more chance of seeing The Invisible Man at the World Cup Finals!

Young Almoez Ali came off the pitch looking very dejected, and sluggishly made his way to the dressing room.

'I've never played so badly before at the Finals,' he sighed.

'Oh,' answered a fellow Qatari player. 'You've played before, have you?'

What do you call an Englishman at a world cup final?

A referee.

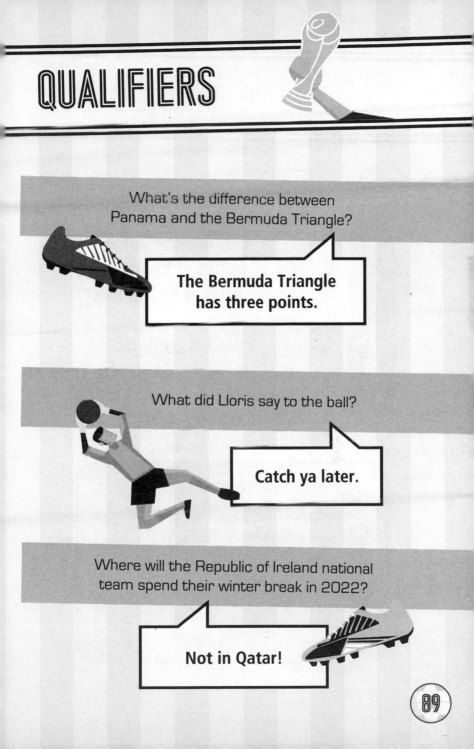

What's the difference between Panama and the Bermuda Triangle?

**The Bermuda Triangle has three points.**

What did Lloris say to the ball?

**Catch ya later.**

Where will the Republic of Ireland national team spend their winter break in 2022?

**Not in Qatar!**

**What do you call an Englishman holding a bottle of champagne after a World Cup?**

*A waiter.*

**What do you call twenty-two millionaires around a TV watching the World Cup final?**

*The Argentina national team.*

# QUALIFIERS

**Why did the Adidas Telstar ball keep shouting?**

*He got a kick out of it.*

• • • • • • • • •

**Why are Panama so bad at geometry?**

*Because they never have any points.*

• • • • • • • • •

**What happens when the US national team crosses the halfway line against Honduras?**

*They score a goal!*

Why do swimmers make
for dirty football players?

They dive a lot.

What's the best thing about
the Switzerland team?

I don't know, but the
flag is a big plus.

Why did the referee wear two
watches to the World Cup final?

He thought that extra
time would be needed!

# QUALIFIERS

Why is the Lusail Iconic Stadium always so windy on match day?

Because it's filled with 80,000 fans.

Why do Alexis Sánchez and his teammates like to wrap up when they play?

Because it's Chile outside.

Why did Italy's midfielder refuse to move all game?

His manager told him to be the anchor-man.

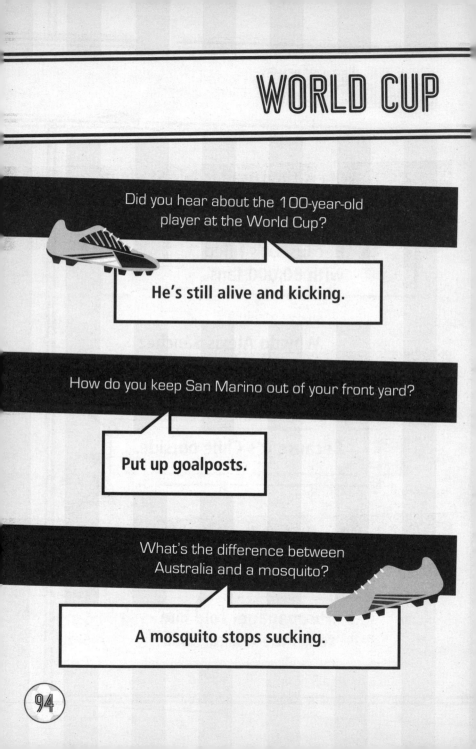

Did you hear about the 100-year-old player at the World Cup?

**He's still alive and kicking.**

How do you keep San Marino out of your front yard?

**Put up goalposts.**

What's the difference between Australia and a mosquito?

**A mosquito stops sucking.**

What do you call it when Cristiano Ronaldo wears a bucket hat, beanie and a cap, and then makes them disappear?

**A hat-trick!**

What's Argentina forward Messi's favourite spice?

**Nutmeg.**

Croatian manager:
Why didn't you turn up to the game last week?

**Croatian striker: You asked me to be an Outside Forward and that's what I was doing!**

How many appearances does
Tomáš Souček have for his country?

**I'm not sure I'll have to Czech!**

*Martin Tyler:* **I've been told that
England's latest centre-back
trained with the Red Arrows.**

*Gary Neville:* **Well, she's
great in the air!**

Did you hear about the Icelandic
centre-back who couldn't swim?

**They gave her the captain's armband.**

# QUALIFIERS

*Scottish team skipper:*
**We've been terrible, coach,
how can we raise our game?**

*Scottish manager:* **Practise
at the top of Ben Nevis?**

**Why are Portugal better than Brazil?**

**They have twice as much Silva!**

*Teacher:* **And why were you
late for school today, Nuha?**

*Nuha:* **I was dreaming about
the World Cup Final and
they went into extra time.**

Did you hear about the Dutch winger who fell in love with the pitch?

He couldn't stop hugging the touchline.

Do you know why they call our goalie the sleeper keeper?

He's always caught napping.

Why did the defender protest his red card despite committing a horrible foul?

He thought it was okay because it was in injury time.

A tourist visiting London stopped a woman carrying a football and asked, 'How do I get to Wembley?'

'Practise!' she replied.

**Megan Rapinoe:**
Why are you wearing sharp teeth and a bushy tail to practice?

**Alex Morgan:**
The gaffer said she wanted me to be a fox in the box!

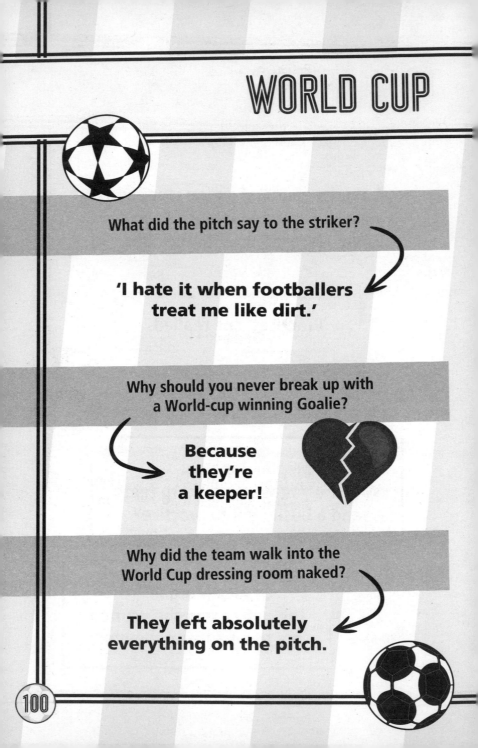

What did the pitch say to the striker?

**'I hate it when footballers treat me like dirt.'**

Why should you never break up with a World-cup winning Goalie?

**Because they're a keeper!**

Why did the team walk into the World Cup dressing room naked?

**They left absolutely everything on the pitch.**

# QUALIFIERS

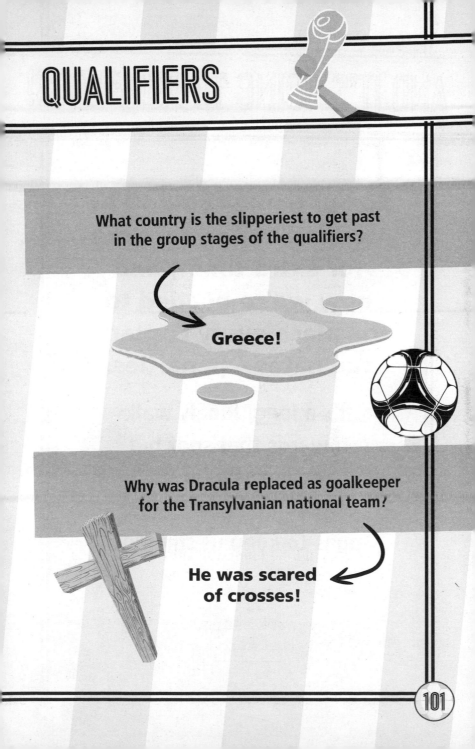

What country is the slipperiest to get past in the group stages of the qualifiers?

**Greece!**

Why was Dracula replaced as goalkeeper for the Transylvanian national team?

**He was scared of crosses!**

# AND IT'S GOING TO PUNALTIES!

**So our game couldn't be decided in normal time (or extra time!) and now we're headed to the place every England fan hates – penalties.**

It's a long, lonely walk towards that spot but fortunately for us, we've got some playful puns to keep us smiling.

When Lionel plays with Neymar and Mbappé at Paris, things are going to get Messi!

A man appeared in court charged with trying to set fire to Everton's main stand. When questioned by the judge, he said he had a burning interest in football.

The footballer was fuming when he was given Velcro boots. What a rip-off!

*I didn't know who had the ball, and then, it hit me!*

**Heathrow F.C. sued the airline company for losing their luggage on a European night. Sadly, they lost the case.**

Seven days of non-stop football can make one weak.

Football is just one habit I will never kick.

The striker who hadn't scored all season wore flop-flops in the changing rooms. He had two left feet.

# AND IT'S GOING

A friend I knew played for
a team called the Musketeers.
They started the season with three
wins and a draw, all 4-1 and one 4-all.

Even though Danny has
left Southampton, it seems
they're flying without Ings.

Eden Hazard is going be the most dangerous Belgian at Qatar 2022.

With regular exorcise, the ghoul-scorer was able to stay fit for the game.

My computer's got the 'Bad-Goalie Virus'. It can't save anything.

The goalie was described as a player who loved boats, because every time he had the ball, he'd give it a long punt down field.

Spurs are doing so badly that Manager of the Month isn't an award for them. It's an appointment!

# TO PUNALTIES!

The other day I heard about this fumbled exorcism. The Goalie just about retained possession!

They say Tottenham's new stadium hasn't got a single flaw. I wonder how any of the teammates play on it.

David Moyes taught West Ham DIY so they could Hammer their opponents.

109

Kepa Arrizabalaga always saw himself as a player who liked to think outside the box.

Unfortunately for him, that meant the end of his career as a goalkeeper.

• • • • • • • • •

Paul Pogba particularly loves watching football matches when he's getting his hair done.

The coverage is the same, but the highlights are even better.

CAN'T GET ENOUGH OF
ULTIMATE FOOTBALL
HEROES?

**Check out heroesfootball.com
for quizzes, games, and competitions!**

**Plus join the Ultimate Football Heroes
Fan Club to score exclusive content
and be the first to hear about
new books and events.
heroesfootball.com/subscribe/**